THE DINOSAUR THAT POOPED A SUPERHERO!

Tom Fletcher and Dougie Poynter
Illustrated by Garry Parsons

PUFFIN

Danny and Dino were off to the city
to see the spectactular sights:
the people, the shops and all the skyscrapers
that soared to incredible heights.

THE DINOSAUR THAT POOPED A SUPERHERO!

For Buzz, Buddy & Max – T.F.
For Grub – D.P.
For my superheroes, C&K – G.P.

PUFFIN BOOKS

UK | USA | Canada | Ireland | Australia
India | New Zealand | South Africa

Puffin Books is part of the Penguin Random House group of companies
whose addresses can be found at global.penguinrandomhouse.com.

www.penguin.co.uk   www.puffin.co.uk   www.ladybird.co.uk

Penguin
Random House
UK

First published 2024
002

Copyright © Tom Fletcher and Dougie Poynter, 2024
Illustrated by Garry Parsons
The moral right of the authors has been asserted

Printed in Italy

A CIP catalogue record for this book is available from the British Library

ISBN: 978–0–241–53166–2

All correspondence to:
Puffin Books, Penguin Random House Children's
One Embassy Gardens, 8 Viaduct Gardens, London SW11 7BW

MIX
Paper | Supporting
responsible forestry
FSC® C018179
FSC
www.fsc.org

But everyone knew that the first thing to do
was to find Dino something to eat.
So, they stopped off at Fudgie's – the sweet-shop downtown –
for a stack of his favourite treats.

Danny chose heaps of the hero-shaped sweets,
then queued up with Mummy and Daddy.

But before they could eat, a CRACK ripped the street,

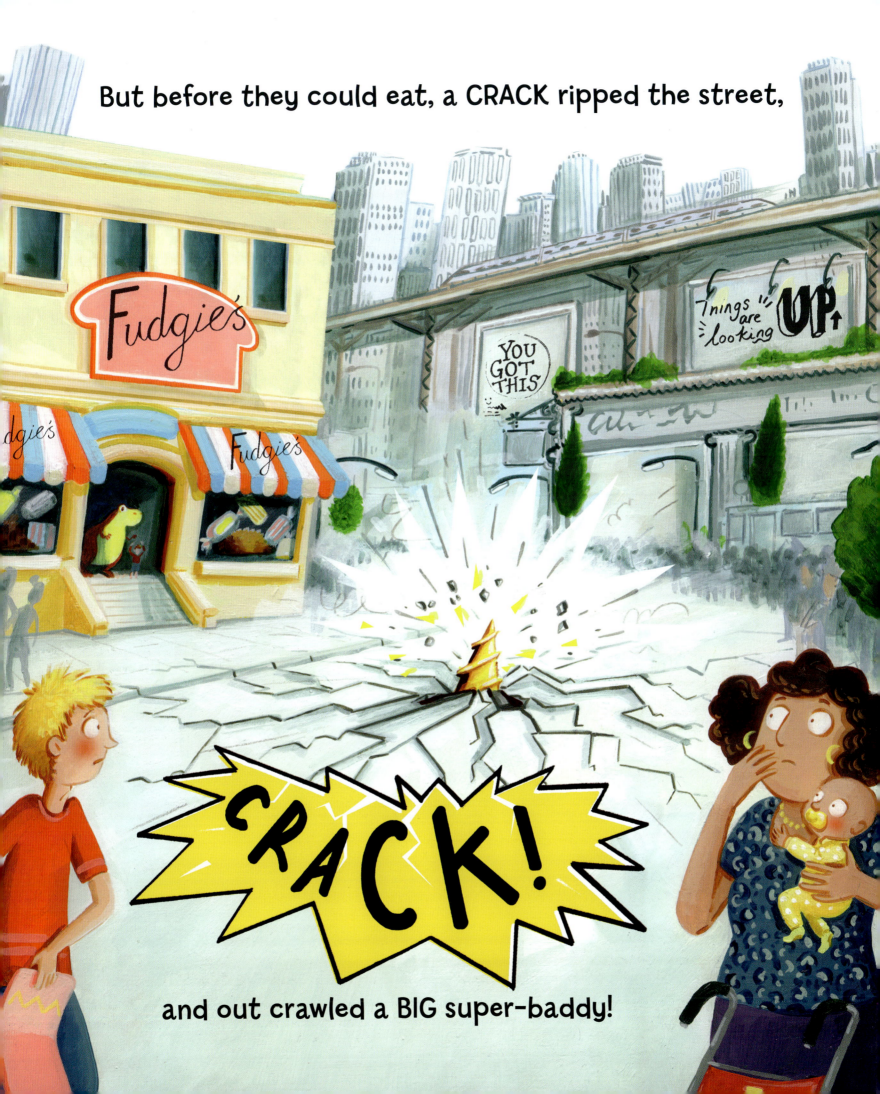

and out crawled a BIG super-baddy!

"I am DESTRUCTO – you'd better beware.
I've come here to ruin this place!"

Then he started to smash, bash and crash down the street
with a mean, angry scowl on his face.

CRACKLE!

"I'm built to DESTROY – it's my FAVOURITE thing.

SNAP!

I'll crush every sight you can see.

Watch as I topple the city with ease – you weaklings will never stop ME!"

BAM!

He dug up some trees and gave them a squeeze,
then he crushed them to dust with his feet!
Dinosaur's gut gave a big, hungry groan
as Destructo destroyed half the street.

Suddenly, up flew a hero called Crush,
who was tough and incredibly strong.
"I'll save the city, no problem!" he cried.
"You won't be around here for long!"

Crush flexed his muscles, all ready to rock,
as Destructo just smirked and said, "Wrong!"
But Dino could hold on no longer and so . . .

. . . in one gulp, the hero was gone!

GULP!

"That was pathetic!" Destructo cried out and continued his villainous mission.

But help was at hand from a hero called Zap,

who was famous for her super vision.

Zap could look straight through a solid brick wall
and see things from miles away, too.

She even beamed lasers to make things explode –
there was nothing Zap's eyes couldn't do!

Zap might have done something very heroic
if Dino had not felt so famished.

He gobbled down Zap in five seconds flat –
now two superheroes had vanished!

"Fools!" cried Destructo, and picked up a train
as his powers grew stronger and stronger.
"What can we do?" shouted Danny to Dino.
"The city won't hold out much longer!"

Just then, out of nowhere, a hero called Zoom
ran over at lightning-fast speed.

"I'll reach the switch, and I'll save us!" he cried . . .
but Dino still needed to feed.

He swallowed down Zoom for a post-dinner snack.
Now three superheroes were eaten!
"YOU'LL NEVER STOP ME!" the baddy cried out.
"Destructo will never be beaten!"

Danny started to cry. He started to sob.
He started to howl, wail and bawl.
With no heroes left, who could save them from doom?
There would soon be no city at all!

But with three superheroes inside of his gut,
Dino knew just what to do.
To make sure Destructo was beaten for good,
the dinosaur needed to . . .

POO!

A giant explosion of poo flooded out,
like a high-pressure super-poo shower.

Crush, Zap and Zoom were still inside Dino's gut,
which made his poo have SUPER POWER!

It zipped through the air flashing lasers around,
and cornered Destructo at speed.
But they needed a hero to finish the job.
Danny cried, "MORE POO'S WHAT WE NEED!"

With one final squeeze, all the heroes shot out –
they were smelly, but ready to win.

"YOU'RE WASTING YOUR TIME," Destructo declared.
"Just you wait!" replied Crush with a grin.

The heroes surrounded the villain at once
and reached the big switch that controlled him.

They changed it from "Villain" to "Nicer than nice".
"Now clear up this city!" they told him.

The city was saved, the baddy was beaten
and everyone gave a big cheer.
Then they rushed back to Fudgie's and filled up their bags
with enough yummy treats for a year!

And just when you thought
all the pooping was done . . .

Dino swallowed the sweet-shop
and pooped it for fun!